Hog Music

by M. C. Helldorfer

illustrated by S. D. Schindler

Viking

For Colby, Jane, and Sally—
traveling to and from
with lots to share in between.

—M.C.H.

To Bob, Nancy, and Megan

—S.D.S.

VIKING
Published by the Penguin Group
Penguin Putnam Books for Young Readers, 345 Hudson Street, New York, New York 10014, U.S.A.
Penguin Books Ltd, 27 Wrights Lane, London W8 5TZ, England
Penguin Books Australia Ltd, Ringwood, Victoria, Australia
Penguin Books Canada Ltd, 10 Alcorn Avenue, Toronto, Ontario, Canada M4V 3B2
Penguin Books (N.Z.) Ltd, 182-190 Wairau Road, Auckland 10, New Zealand

Penguin Books Ltd, Registered Offices: Harmondsworth, Middlesex, England

First published in 2000 by Viking, a division of Penguin Putnam Books for Young Readers.

5 7 9 10 8 6 4

Text copyright © M. C. Helldorfer, 2000
Illustrations copyright © S. D. Schindler, 2000
All rights reserved

The art was painted in watercolor and gouache on parchment paper.

LIBRARY OF CONGRESS CATALOGING-IN-PUBLICATION DATA
Helldorfer, Mary-Claire, date-
Hog music / by M.C. Helldorfer ; illustrated by S.D. Schindler.
p. cm.
Summary: Travelers along the National Road help make sure that the birthday gift that
Lucy's great aunt has sent makes it all the way from Maryland to her family's farm in Illinois.
ISBN 0-670-87182-6
[1. Frontier and pioneer life—Fiction. 2. Voyages and travels—Fiction. 3. Gifts—Fiction.]
I. Title. II. Schindler, S. D., ill.
PZ7.H37418 Ho 2000
[E]21—dc21   99-042059

Printed in Hong Kong
Set in Raleigh and Poppl-Pontifex

About This Book

In the first half of the nineteenth century, the National Public Road, which began in Maryland, crossed the Allegheny Mountains in Pennsylvania, and eventually reached as far west as the Mississippi Valley, was the main route of travel between east and west in the United States. Davy Crockett, Andrew Jackson, Abraham Lincoln, and P. T. Barnum all traveled this road and got as mud-spattered as the less famous folks: the teamsters hauling goods; drovers with their hogs, sheep, and cattle; mail coach drivers; preachers; entertainers and circus performers; journalists; curious British travelers; and families starting a new life in the West.

At the Smithsonian Museum of American History and at its Postal Museum, my imaginings about life in the 1840s—things like Conestogas, coaches, carriages, and crockery—became real. Merritt Ierley's history, *Traveling the National Road*, contains some of the funny and often moving accounts of those who took the journey. These memoirs, along with the letters of women who had come to the plains and felt far away from the mothers and sisters they had left behind, inspired my story.

Lucy looked up at the big blue wagon with bright red wheels. Papa hitched up the horses. Mama pitched one last pile of hay into the Conestoga. The wagon was crammed with most everything the family needed for a new home and a farm of their own in a place called Illinois.

"Wish you'd come with us, Aunt Liza," Lucy said.

The old lady shook her head. "Nothing but hog music out there."

Papa gave Lucy a boost into the wagon. She plopped down on the sweet-smelling hay.

"Miss you, Auntie," Lucy called softly.

"Hog music!"

Lucy's family left in early spring. Great Aunt Liza was still fussing the first of October. That day she shopped in Baltimore for a plain straw hat and put it in a plain wooden box with a latch.

"Happy Birthday from Aunt Liza," she wrote. She left out *love*.

Then she gave the gift to her old friend Dr. Edwards, who was heading west by mail coach.

Whooeee! That stagecoach headed west—and
up and down and left and right. It leaped over
rocks and dropped into ruts and swerved around stumps. It left
the doctor's hat smashed against the ceiling, his cigar between his
feet, and two ladies in his lap.

Who'd notice when a little baggage strap broke?

Silas Turner, pushing a handcart along the road, found Aunt Liza's box. "Lucy Owen, Vandalia, Illinois," he read, and put it in his cart.

Now the road was growing dark, the moon rising like a shiny supper plate over the mountains. Hungry wagoners unhitched their horses in fields close to a tavern. Cattle drovers carried their bedrolls inside. Hogs in nearby pens made frosty grinding music.

"Time to work," said Silas.

He was good at painting miniature portraits, pictures that were tiny as buttons. Later, when the tavern owner played the fiddle, Silas gave dance lessons. Then he fell asleep by the fire with all the other men. Phew—one smelled as bad as a goat.

When Silas awoke, Aunt Liza's wooden box lay open. Something had eaten the brim of the straw hat. Silas felt so bad, he placed in the box one of his own little paintings, a fine portrait of his grandma's pet hog.

A wagoner named McBride added some
coffee beans and offered to take the box west.

McBride's team of eight hauled a heavy load up and
down the mountains of Maryland and Pennsylvania and
across a strip of old Virginia. They were halfway through
Ohio when McBride heard a terrible rumbling.

He snapped his whip. Too late! The bridge splintered
beneath his wagon's weight. Coffee barrels
and tobacco floated in the creek.

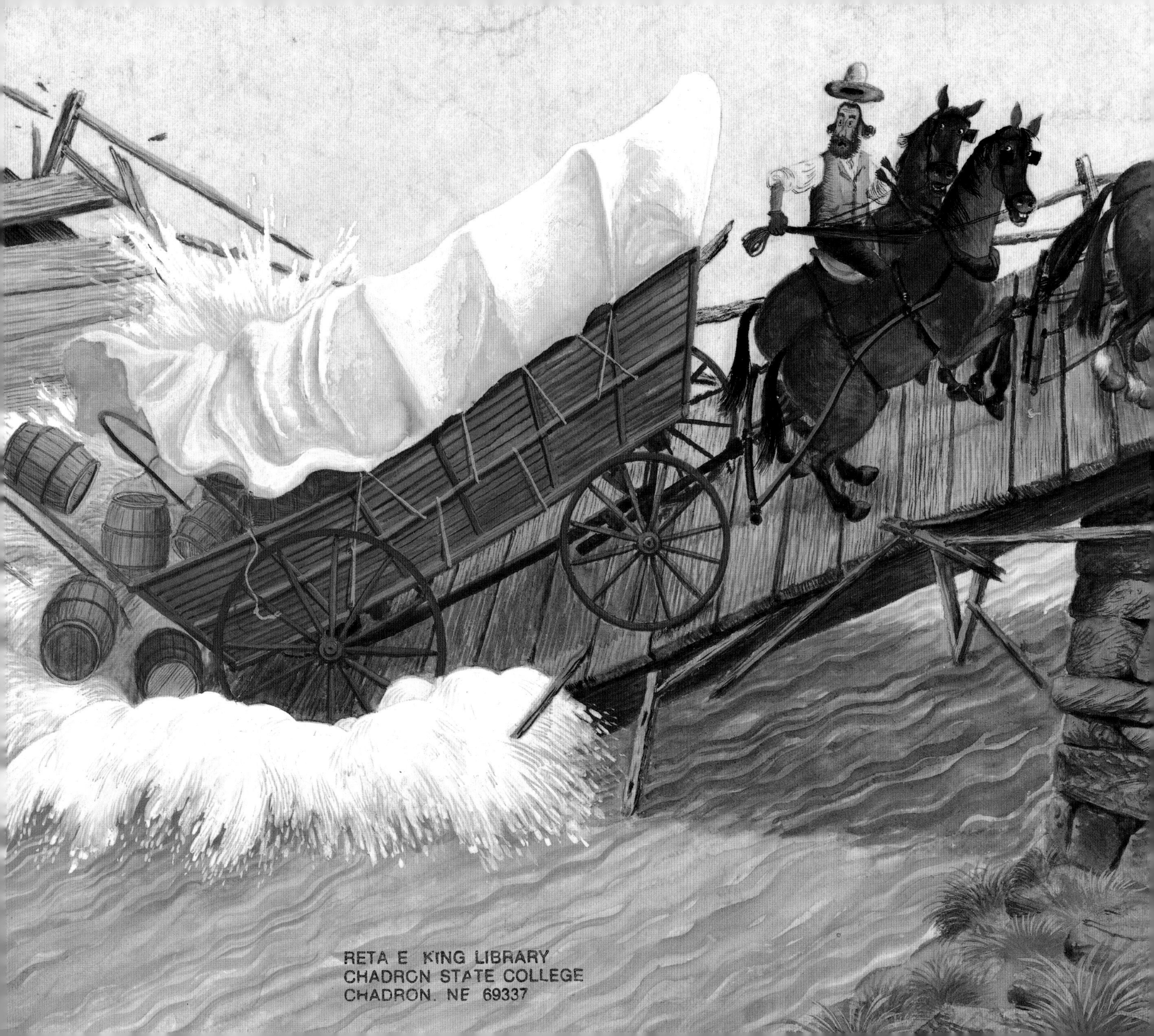

Several miles downstream, a farm boy was fishing. Young Henry caught nothing that day but a wooden box labeled "Lucy Owen, Vandalia, Illinois."

The only gift Henry liked in the box was the little picture of the hog, so he added one of his own clay marbles.

When he and his mama took the box to the country store, the owner, Mr. Marryat, added a silk ribbon.

Mrs. Marryat, who was heading to Indiana to see her sister, carried the gift westward.

Mudfly Marryat, that's what neighbors called her in Ohio. When she drove her carriage, mud flew, birds flew—everything with feet, wheels, or wings flew out of her way. But the farmer from Indiana didn't see how fast that whirlwind was coming down the road.

Whoa!

Up-a-daisy!

When Mrs. Marryat righted her carriage and reloaded her pickle jars, wallpaper rolls, ax, whiskey, sewing basket, and pistol, she left something in the grass.

Luckily, Mr. Jupiter's Traveling Show of Wonders was passing through. A trained monkey found the box and brought it to his owner, the beautiful Rosa May.

"Poor Lucy Owen," Rosa clucked when she opened the gift.

"She needs something special for her birthday."

Curling a long, shimmery peacock feather,

Rosa placed it in the wooden box.

The circus wagons rolled on, but that night, when Rosa was asleep, the monkey opened up Jupiter's Trunk of Wonders. He swiped from it a jar labeled "George Washington's Baby Teeth," and emptied the whole thing into Aunt Liza's box. Then, just for the fun of it, he threw the gift out of the wagon. It landed in a ditch . . .

. . . where it was found by Lewis Munger, who was driving his hogs to market, whistling to much snorting and grunting music. Lewis thought the tiny picture of the hog a fine work of art. He carried the box eastward till he met someone he trusted to take it west again to Lucy Owen, Vandalia, Illinois.

The Reverend Godby, searching for a promised land on which to build his church, carried the gift to the border of Illinois. But when he came upon the very tree and rock he had seen in his dreams, he stopped. On the back of Aunt Liza's birthday note, he wrote a quick message to Lucy, then gave the box to a peddler.

Now, this peddler, Caleb Faux, planned to sell the box and everything inside. But when he saw the silk ribbon, he thought of his own pretty Lucy at home.

He added one of his special beauty products and took the gift as far as the general store and post office of Vandalia, Illinois.

Which was where Lucy, Papa, and Mama came every few weeks for supplies and news from home. Lucy opened the box right away. She read Aunt Liza's birthday message, then the odd writing on the other side of the note. "Creator of us all!" it said. "Manifold indeed are thy wondrous gifts!"

Indeed, Lucy was filled with wonder when she saw the many gifts in the box. Papa said that he hoped Aunt Liza was feeling all right.

Mama helped Lucy write a thank you note. They posted it from the store.

Several weeks later, when Aunt Liza received Lucy's note, she began wondering herself. She showed it to Dr. Edwards, who had just returned from his trip with sorry news about losing the gift.

Dear Aunt Liza,

Thank you for the birthday surprise. The little hat is exactly the right size. And I love the marble.

"Marble?" said Dr. Edwards.

And I needed the ribbon.

"Ribbon?"

The peacock feather is beautiful!

"Peacock feather!" the doctor and Aunt Liza exclaimed, looking at each other.

And I'm sure the teeth will bring me good luck.

"Merciful heavens!" said Aunt Liza, fanning herself with the letter.

Papa says thank you for the coffee beans.

Aunt Liza frowned.

Mama says thank you for the Moondazzle Face Cream.

Aunt Liza's cheeks began to redden.

But most of all we love the tiny painting of the hog. I think there must be thousands and thousands and thousands of hogs between you and us. But we have only one. On our farm we have corn, prairie grass, and wild flowers. We have only wind music.

"Wind music," Aunt Liza repeated softly.

I miss you. I wish you would come.

Well, the old woman sat looking at the letter for a long time. "Perhaps," she said at last, "I should take the stage and see if I can have as many adventures as one wooden box."

Which she did.

For Lucy, it was the best gift.